P9-CDC-790

the RATTLEBANG P·I·C·N·I·C

by MARGARET MAHY

pictures by STEVEN KELLOGG

Dial Books for Young Readers

New York

BΊ I   14.99   2/95

Published by Dial Books for Young Readers
A Division of Penguin Books USA Inc.
375 Hudson Street / New York, New York 10014

Text copyright © 1994 by Margaret Mahy
Pictures copyright © 1994 by Steven Kellogg
All rights reserved
Typography by Jane Byers Bierhorst
Printed in the U.S.A.
First Edition
1 2 3 4 5 6 7 8 9 10

The full-color artwork was prepared using ink
and pencil line and watercolor washes.

Library of Congress Cataloging in Publication Data

Mahy, Margaret.
The rattlebang picnic / by Margaret Mahy
pictures by Steven Kellogg.—1st ed.
p.   cm.
Summary: The McTavishes, their seven
children, and Granny McTavish take their
old rattlebang of a car on a picnic up
Mt. Fogg and have an exciting adventure.
ISBN 0-8037-1318-5 (trade).
ISBN 0-8037-1319-3 (lib. bdg.)
[1. Picnicking—Fiction.
2. Automobiles—Fiction.]
I. Kellogg, Steven, ill. II. Title.
III. Title: Rattlebang picnic.
PZ7.M2773Rat   1994
[E]—dc20   93-36294   CIP   AC

To Penny and Bridget, who have been on so
many rattlebang picnics with me
M.M.

To Laurie and Sam, with love
S.K.

When Jack McTavish married sweet Marion McGillicuddy, they counted their money and talked things over seriously.

"We can afford either a wonderful, speedy car that never breaks down, or we can have lots of children," said Jack McTavish. "What a pity we can't have both."

"Perhaps we can have a few children—just six or seven—if we make do with an old car," suggested the new Mrs. McTavish.

"That's a good idea!" cried Mr. McTavish, looking pleased. "We'll have seven children and get by with an old rattlebang."

So the McTavishes had seven children

and drove an old rattlebang.

"You have done the right thing," said Jack McTavish's mother, Granny McTavish.

She liked having grandchildren.

"We can all go on picnics in the rattlebang, and I will make pancakes and pizzas for us to eat."

Now Granny McTavish was a good grandmother, but she was not a very good cook. Her pies and pizzas were tougher than old boots. The trouble was, she always baked everything for an hour or two at a very low temperature and it toughened things up.

You could use her pies, pizzas, and pancakes as Frisbees, or bowl them along the beach. But you just couldn't bite into them, even if your teeth were very strong.

One day Marion McTavish—who was famous for being adventurous—said, "We've often been on picnics to the beach or to the river. For our next picnic let's drive to the very tip-top of Mount Fogg."

"Yes, yes, yes," called the seven McTavish children and Granny McTavish in one voice, for they were all adventurous as well.

However, Jack McTavish looked grave. "I'm not too sure that's a good idea," he said. "The road's winding and rocky, and we only have the old rattlebang to get us there. Pieces keep dropping off it."

"I'm sure it will be just fine," cried Marion McTavish. "We're longing to climb the mountain and swim in the hot springs."
"All right. We'll risk it," Jack McTavish decided.

So on the next picnic day Mr. McTavish, Mrs. McTavish, the seven little McTavishes, and Granny McTavish piled into the old rattlebang and set off for Mount Fogg.

It was a beautiful morning. A plume of pure white cloud floated around the top of the mountain. The old rattlebang struggled up the winding, rocky road—bumping and banging and backfiring—then stopped right beside the hot springs.

Everyone plunged into the warm water and swam happily up and down. Later they dried themselves by jumping over the hot-air geysers that blew between the rocks.

"This is perfect!" said Mr. McTavish, setting out the lunch. "I can't think why more people don't picnic here."

The only disappointment was the pizza Granny McTavish had insisted on making. It was so hard that it bent the picnic knife.

Even banging it with sharp rocks failed to chip any pieces free.

After an hour of hard work the little McTavishes had only managed to grind a hole in the middle of it. Apart from that, the pizza was quite unyielding.

"Well, it probably wouldn't be good for us anyway," said sensible Mrs. McTavish. "We shall make do with cupcakes and apples."

So after a delicious cupcake-and-apple lunch, they stretched out in the sun to rest before setting out for the top of Mount Fogg.

As they dozed, they were surprised to feel the mountain jiggling and rumbling beneath them, as if it too were digesting an agreeable meal.

Suddenly there was a great volcanic roar. The ground shook violently. The white cloud surrounding the peak turned gray and then black, and red-hot lava poured down the mountainside.

"Quick, everyone, into the car!" cried Mr. McTavish.

So they all piled into the old rattlebang and set off down the rocky, winding road—bumping and banging and backfiring—while the red-hot lava burbled furiously after them.

"The car is going very well for an old rattlebang," said Granny McTavish.

But just as she spoke, the car gave a sickening lurch. A wheel had fallen off the rattlebang. It went bowling swiftly down the rocky road ahead of them, struck a stone, and leaped out in- to limitless space. Down, down, down it fell, becoming smaller and smaller until it vanished completely. Behind them the ten McTavishes could hear the sinister hiss of the red-hot lava flowing toward them.

"No screaming now. Everyone think quickly!" Mr. McTavish said.

"Granny's pizza!" his seven children cried together. "Put Granny's pizza on the old rattlebang."

Hastily Mr. and Mrs. McTavish jacked up the old rattlebang, trying not to notice the red-hot lava creeping closer and closer.

Then Mr. McTavish banged the pizza onto the axle, using an iron mallet (which they always carried in case of emergencies), while Mrs. McTavish rubbed the axle with what was left of the picnic butter so that the pizza would spin around smoothly. By now the red-hot lava was very, very close.

"All right!" said Jack McTavish briskly. "Let's give it a whirl!"

Everybody piled back into the old rattlebang as the red-hot lava rose behind them like a tidal wave.

The engine coughed and sputtered—then burst to life. Off they went—bumping and banging and backfiring—down the winding, rocky road, leaving the volcano and red-hot lava far behind. The old rattlebang may have looked a little strange with a pizza in place of a wheel, but none of the McTavishes cared about that.

"How wise we were to have seven children instead of a speedy new car!" exclaimed Mr. and Mrs. McTavish, smiling at each other.

And how wise I was to cook that pizza for an hour and a half at a low temperature, thought Granny McTavish.

MT. FOGG
SCENIC
OVERLOOK

"What a wonderful picnic," the seven McTavish children murmured to one another. "Perhaps for our next picnic day we can all pile into the old rattlebang and go to Tornado Valley. That would be fun too!"

And they banged and bumped and backfired all the way home in perfect safety.